Mess on the Rocks

Written by Zoë Clarke
Illustrated by Nathalie Ortega

Collins

It is a big mess.

Get it in the bins.

Pick up the big mess ...

locks, socks, bags and tins.

I pick up the mess.

I toss lots of tins.

I fill a bag up.

Toss bags in the bins.

Dip nets in the rocks.

It is lots of fun.

I hop on the moss.

Gulls hop in the sun.

/b/

ll

After reading

Letters and Sounds: Phase 2

Word count: 60

Focus phonemes: /g/ /o/ /e/ /u/ /r/ /h/ /b/ /f/ /l/ ck, ll, ss

Common exception words: a, of, the, I, is, and

Curriculum links: Understanding the World: The World

Early learning goals: Understanding: answer "how" and "why" questions about their experiences and in response to stories or events; Reading: children use phonic knowledge to decode regular words and read them aloud accurately, read some common irregular words, demonstrate understanding when talking with others about what they have read

Developing fluency

- Your child may enjoy hearing you read the book.
- Ask your child to read the speech bubbles on pages 3 and 9 with lots of expression. You may wish to model reading one of them first.

Phonic practice

- Look at page 5 together. Ask your child to find two words that rhyme. (*locks*, *socks*) Say the middle sound of each word together. Can they think of any other words that rhyme with **locks** and **socks**? (e.g. *rocks, docks*)
- Now do the same with pages 11 and 13, **fun** and **sun**. (e.g. *run*)
- Look at the "I spy sounds" pages (14–15). Say the sounds together. How many items can your child spot that have the /b/ sound in their name? (e.g. *bird, bin, bag, bottle, banana, bear, box, bell*)
- Can they find any words that end with the letters "ll"? (e.g. *doll, gull, fill*)

Extending vocabulary

- Read page 9 to your child. Can they think of another word that could have been used instead of **toss**? (*throw, put*)
- Read page 10 to your child. Can they think of another word that could have been used instead of **rocks**? (*stones, boulders*)